Arthur and the Double Dare

A Marc Brown ARTHUR Chapter Book

Arthur and the Double Dare

Text by Stephen Krensky
Based on a teleplay by Kathy Waugh

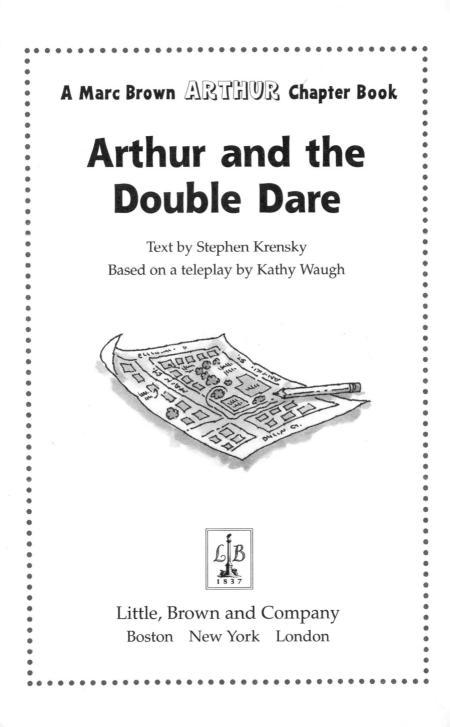

Little, Brown and Company
Boston   New York   London

First Edition

The characters and events portrayed in this book are fictitious. Any
similarity to real persons, living or dead, is coincidental and not intended
by the author.

Arthur® is a registered trademark of Marc Brown.

Text has been reviewed and assigned a reading level by Laurel S. Ernst,
M.A., Teachers College, Columbia University, New York, New York;
reading specialist, Chappaqua, New York.

Library of Congress Cataloging-in-Publication Data

Krensky, Stephen.
  Arthur and the double dare / text by Stephen Krensky ; based on a
teleplay by Kathy Waugh. — 1st ed.
    p. cm. — (A Marc Brown Arthur chapter book ; 25)
  Summary: Unhappy about how much homework they have to do,
Arthur and his friends dare each other to skip school.
    ISBN 0-316-12264-5 (hc) / ISBN 0-316-12087-1 (pb)
    [1. Friendship — Fiction. 2. Schools — Fiction. 3. Aardvark — Fiction.
4. Animals — Fiction.] I. Arthur (Television program) II. Title.

PZ7.K883 Aqd 2002
[Fic] — dc21   2001050476

                    10 9 8 7 6 5 4 3 2 1

                            WOR (hc)
                           COM-MO (pb)

Printed in the United States of America

For Steven and Helen Kellogg

Chapter 1

. . . .

Arthur, Buster, Francine, and the Brain were sitting in the tree house one day after school. They all looked tired, especially Arthur, who was fishing a bunch of papers out of his backpack.

"I can't believe how much homework Mr. Ratburn gave us," he said, pulling out one page after another. "I'll never get to watch any TV tonight."

"No kidding," said Buster. "Any other night it might not matter so much, but tonight's the final showdown between Dark Bunny and the Sixty-Foot Squid."

Francine nodded. "Will he or won't he get eaten by a giant clam and —"

"Get digested by clam juice?" Buster finished for her.

The Brain sighed. "And we won't get to see it, not with all this work."

"It's so unfair," said Arthur. "Mr. Ratburn gets to make all the decisions himself. Sometimes, I think *we* should get to decide whether we get homework or not."

"Yeah!" said Buster. "I like that idea. I like it a lot. I'd like to make that decision all the time."

"Which is exactly why we don't get to," the Brain pointed out.

"Still," said Arthur, "we should get some choice. One of these days, I'm just not going to do my homework."

"Impossible," said Buster. "How could you ever face Mr. Ratburn?"

"I don't know," Arthur admitted. He

straightened up his shoulders and took a deep breath. "I just wouldn't go to school, maybe. If I'm not at school, I don't have to worry about homework."

Francine laughed. "Oh, right. You, skip school? Come on, you're too much of a scaredy-cat."

"I am not!" Arthur insisted. "There's not a scaredy-cat bone in my body. I could skip school in a minute." He tried to snap his fingers. "Like . . . like that!"

Francine snorted. "Oh, yeah?"

"Yeah!"

"Okay, then," said Francine. "I dare you!"

The other kids gasped.

"Wow!" said Buster. "She dared you, Arthur."

"So?" Arthur shrugged.

"It's a dare," said Buster. "Now you have to do it."

"No, I don't," said Arthur. "That's silly."

"Yes, you do," said the Brain. "It's the rule."

"What rule?"

"You know," said the Brain, "*the* rule. I don't make them up, I just call them."

"Oh, really?" said Arthur. He turned to Francine. "So just because you dared me, I have to do what you say?"

Francine nodded.

"And that's true for anyone?"

"Yes," Francine said.

"Fine," said Arthur. "In that case, I dare you back!"

Francine jerked back her head. "But you can't just —"

"Oh, yes, he can," said the Brain. "The rule is quite specific on that point."

Well . . . ," Francine went on, "well, then I dare Buster!"

"Me?" Buster's jaw dropped. "How did I get into this?"

"It doesn't matter, Buster," the Brain informed him. "Once you're dared, you're dared."

"Well, then I dare you, too!" cried Buster.

Now it was the Brain's turn to look shocked. "This is serious, guys. Very serious."

Chapter 2

● ● ● ● ● ● ● ● ● ● ● ●

An hour later, the kids climbed down from the tree house. There had been a lot of arguing and shouting in that hour, leaving both Arthur and Francine with very red faces.

But everything was finally settled. Now, as they all gathered at the base of the tree, the Brain held up a map he had drawn of the neighborhood.

"Okay," he said. "Here's how we'll do it. Normally, we walk to school in a straight line down Main Street." He traced the route on the map with his finger. "But tomorrow we'll each make a right at this

bush just after the Sugar Bowl. That's our rendezvous point."

"Our what?" asked Buster.

"The place where we meet. And then . . . ummmm . . . once everyone gets there, we'll turn right again."

"Where will we go?" asked Buster.

"I don't know," the Brain admitted. "But we won't go to school. The double-daring rule is very clear about that. No, no, Arthur, don't say anything. We can wait till tomorrow to decide our next step."

Arthur wasn't so sure of that.

Arthur hacked his way through the jungle with his bright steel machete. As the crickets chirped in the background, he dodged under a giant cobweb and leapt over a snake slithering across the path.

Buster, Francine, and the Brain were behind him.

"Where are we?" asked Buster, slapping at a mosquito.

"In the jungle," said Arthur.

"I suspect Buster is aware of that," said the Brain. "He means where exactly." He examined his compass. "According to my calculations, we're somewhere north of Greenland." He looked around. "But I don't believe that's right."

"Oh, really?" said Francine. "You needed a compass to tell you that?"

"We're exactly in the jungle," said Arthur, taking another swipe at a vine. "That's all you need to know."

"Why don't you just admit it?" said Francine. "We're lost and we're never going to get out of here."

"That should make you happy," said Arthur. "If we stay in the jungle, you'll never have to go to school again."

Arthur shook his head to clear the vision from his mind.

"That's not much of a plan," Francine said.

"It's the best one we have," the Brain reminded her.

Arthur sighed. "I really don't think we should do this," he said.

"Are you starting again?" asked Francine. "Because if you are . . ."

"Nobody's starting," insisted the Brain, staring at Arthur.

"Okay, okay," said Arthur.

"It was your idea, after all," said Francine.

"That's not true," said Arthur. "Besides, you dared me first. I was only wishing, and then you made a big —"

Buster made a T with his hands. "Time out," he said. "I thought we agreed not to argue anymore."

"I only agreed if Arthur agreed," said Francine. "So if he's unagreeing, I'm unagreeing, too. Actually, I'm unagreeing first, so he has to unagree with me — if he wants to."

"Look, guys," the Brain cut in, "however it happened, it's out of our hands now. We've all been dared . . . and that's that."

Chapter 3

• • • • • • • • • • • •

At the dinner table that night, Arthur didn't have much to say. Even when Baby Kate turned her head sideways and picked a french fry off his plate, he didn't notice.

D.W. stared at him.

"Mom," said Arthur, "D.W. is giving me the evil eye."

"I am not," said D.W. "I'm just curious. Your face looks all funny, so there must be a reason. What are you thinking about?"

"None of your business!"

"Arthur . . . ," said Mom.

"D.W.," said Dad, "maybe you could turn your attention away from your brother and toward those brussels sprouts. I think they're feeling a bit neglected."

"Do I have to? Arthur is much more interesting than brussels sprouts." She paused. "Well, sometimes."

Arthur made a face at her.

A little later Arthur sat on the couch in the living room watching TV.

D.W. stuck her head in the doorway. "Is it safe to come in?"

"Yeah, sure — it's a commercial, anyway."

D.W. hopped onto the couch. "So has the clam eaten Dark Bunny yet?"

"Yup."

"Was it really disgusting?" D.W. asked.

"I guess so."

"Good," said D.W. "So are you going to tell me what's bothering you?"

Arthur frowned. "Will you quit it, D.W.? I don't look guilty."

"I didn't say you looked guilty," said D.W.

"Oh. Well, that's what you were thinking. I look completely the opposite — completely . . . not guilty."

Mom stuck her head in.

"Don't you have any homework, Arthur?"

He shook his head. "Um, I've done everything I need to."

"All right." She gave him a long look. "If you need to talk, you know where to find me."

Arthur nodded, but he wasn't really paying attention. After sitting for a few more minutes, he went to bed early.

However, he had trouble sleeping.

"No, no . . . ," he mumbled, tossing and turning.

Arthur was trapped inside a giant clam. He

could barely see out through the curvy opening.

"Where am I?" he asked.

"Well, you're certainly not at school, are you?" said the Evil Clam. Its slimy voice, dripping with contempt, seemed to come from everywhere at once.

"I . . . no . . . but I want to be!"

"Are we inside a clam?" said Buster, who had suddenly appeared at Arthur's side. "Boy, it really stinks in here."

Arthur looked at him in surprise. "Where did you come from?"

"Don't ask me," said Buster. "It's your dream. But I know one thing — I'm leaving."

He knocked on the clamshell. "Hey you, Evil Clam Guy, let us out!"

"Too late for that," said the Evil Clam. "You took a wrong turn at that bush back there and now . . ."

A wave of disgusting liquid washed over their feet.

"Yuck!" said Arthur. "What's that?"

Buster took a sniff. "It smells like clam juice. I think we're being . . ."

"DIGESTED!" they screamed together.

Chapter 4

● ● ● ● ● ● ● ● ● ● ●

When Arthur awoke the next morning, he opened his eyes and — "Arggghhhh!" he cried.

"There's no need to scream," said D.W., who was staring at him from just inches away. "It's only me."

"D.W., what are you doing here?"

"It's an experiment. Mom kept calling to you. And you kept not answering. So I thought I would come in and see how many times it took before you woke up."

"I didn't sleep very well," Arthur muttered. He rolled over to the side of the bed.

"Now if you've finished experimenting, please get out so I can get dressed."

A few minutes later, Arthur came down to the kitchen. He was dressed and had washed his face, but he still looked half asleep.

"You'd better hurry," said his mother. "You don't want to be late for school."

Arthur yawned as he poured himself some cereal and milk.

Suddenly, D.W. started to laugh.

The milk had spilled over the edge of the bowl onto the table.

"Ha, ha," Arthur said grumpily. He cleaned up the mess and stumbled over to the phone. Then he called Buster.

"Buster? It's me." He yawned again. "I can't go through with it. I don't care if Francine did dare me."

At home in his kitchen, Buster was yawning, too. "I can't go through with it, either," he said. "I'm so tired I just put some bread in the refrigerator to toast. And it's all the fault of this dream I had. There was this giant clam that told me that if I didn't go to school I'd be digested. And all I know is that when a clam tells you to do something, you do it."

"That's so weird," said Arthur. "I had the same dream. And I —"

Arthur stopped because he saw that D.W. was no longer eating her breakfast. She was listening to his every word.

"Go away!" he said. "I'm on the phone."

"It's a free country," said D.W.

"It may be free, but that doesn't mean I won't make you pay later." He cupped his hand over the phone. "Buster," he continued in a whisper, "can you call everyone and tell them the you-know-what is canceled? I can't talk any more right now."

"Can do," said Buster. He hung up and called the Brain.

"Everything's off," he said. "I'll explain more at school."

"Thank goodness," said the Brain. "I had the strangest dream about this clam. . . ."

"Really?" said Buster. "So did I!"

They compared dreams for a minute. "Oh," Buster said suddenly, "I forgot. I have to call Francine. See you later."

But when he dialed Francine, no one answered. *She's probably in the bathroom or something,* he thought. *I'll just leave a message.*

"Buster, you'd better get a move on," said his mother, who was getting ready for work.

"Right," he said. He left the message, hung up the phone, and picked up his backpack. Then he scooted out the door.

"Too many phone calls," he mumbled, hoping he wouldn't be late.

Chapter 5

• • • • • • • • • • •

"All right, class," said Mr. Ratburn, "let's settle down. The bell's going to ring in a minute."

Arthur gulped. As he looked around the room, he saw everyone taking a seat. Everyone, that is, except Francine.

"Brain, where's Francine?" he asked.

The Brain shrugged. "I can't say. I haven't seen her."

Arthur turned around. "Buster," he whispered, "have you seen Francine?"

Buster shook his head.

"I thought you called her," Arthur said.

"I did," Buster said.

"Well, was there any way she didn't understand what you were saying?"

"I don't know."

Arthur frowned. "What do you mean, you don't know?"

"Well," Buster explained, "I didn't actually talk to her. I left a message on her machine."

"You did?" Arthur bit his lip.

"I figured she was in the bathroom or something," Buster went on.

Arthur frowned. It was the "or something" he was worried about.

Francine was worried, too. She had been standing by the bush for almost half an hour. It was not a very interesting bush and didn't give her much to look at. For a while she had been distracted by the kids passing by every few minutes. But now the street was quiet.

"Where are they?" she muttered, looking at her watch. Just because they were skipping school didn't mean they were allowed to be late. After all, *she* had been on time. She had even ignored a ringing phone at her house in order to stay on schedule.

"When I make a promise," she said, "I keep it."

She stared at the ground, shaking her head.

Francine was polishing the armor in her castle when a messenger came rushing in.

"Francine, it's the dragon," he gasped.

"Which dragon?" she asked. "There are so many."

"The green one as big as this castle whose fiery breath can melt rocks."

Francine nodded. "Oh, that dragon. What about him?"

"He's dared you to meet him in single combat." The messenger took a deep breath. "What will you do?"

Francine examined the edge of her sword.
"Meet him, of course. Let's see . . . I'll put him
down for next Thursday. Oh, wait." She looked
at her calendar. "Thursday's no good. That's
when I'm meeting the two-headed giant by the
edge of the forest. He — or is it they? — dared
me first. Find out if the dragon is free on
Wednesday."

The messenger nodded and started to leave.
Then he turned back. "May I ask you something?" he said.

Francine stopped polishing. "Of course."

"How do you do it? I mean, you get one dare
after another. You never turn any down, no
matter how they pile up."

"That's true," said Francine. "But I have no
choice. A dare must be accepted. That's the
rule."

"Can't the rule ever be broken?"

Francine shrugged. "Maybe by some people,
but not by me."

Francine looked at her watch again.

Even if all the boys were late, at least one of them would have arrived by now. "It's nine o'clock already. Shoot. I'm going to kill those guys."

She hesitated for another moment — and then headed off to school as fast as she could.

Chapter 6

• • • • • • • • • • •

"Psssssst!"

Buster flicked his hand at the fly he thought was buzzing around him. Everyone was completing a worksheet Mr. Ratburn had handed out.

"Pssssssssssst!"

Buster flicked his hand again.

"PSSSSSSSSSSSSST!"

Buster looked up to see Francine's head popping up at an open window.

"Hi, Francine," he said.

"Where's Mr. Ratburn?" whispered Francine.

"Out in the hall talking with Mrs. Mac-

Grady about the lunch count." Buster stared at her. "What are you doing out there?"

"What am I doing out *here?* What are you and Arthur and the Brain doing in *there?* I thought we had a deal!"

"We called it off," said Buster. "Didn't you get my message?"

"NO! I waited and waited and waited."

"We're sorry," said Arthur, who was relieved that Francine had at least shown up. "But why haven't you come in?"

"The front door is locked now," Francine said. "I can't get in without ringing the bell. And if I do that, I'll have a lot of explaining to do. I need to get in some other way."

Arthur thought for a moment.

"Meet us at the window outside the boys' bathroom," he told her.

"Okay," she said, and ducked out of sight.

A few minutes later Arthur and Buster entered the boys' bathroom. Arthur quickly walked over to the window in the far wall.

"Wait a minute, Arthur!" said Buster. "Haven't you forgotten something?"

"What's that?" Arthur asked.

"Girls aren't allowed to go into the boys' bathroom," Buster said.

Arthur paused. "Well, that's okay. Francine won't be going in."

"She won't?"

"Nope. She'll only be going out."

"Oh," said Buster. "That's a relief."

Arthur stuck his head out the window and called to Francine, who wasn't sure which window was which.

"Over here!"

Francine ran over and reached up toward the windowsill.

"I'm not tall enough," she said. "You're going to have to help."

Arthur reached down and grabbed her wrists. "Ummmph," he said. "You may not be tall enough, but you're heavy enough."

"Don't just let me hang here!" said Francine. "Pull me up!"

"Buster," Arthur groaned, "I need your help."

"Check." Buster grabbed Arthur by the belt and pulled.

"Ow!" said Arthur. "Not so hard!"

"Arthur!" said Francine. "Pay attention! You're going to drop me."

"I'm doing the best I can," said Arthur. "You're too heavy."

"I am NOT too heavy. I weigh less than you do," Francine said.

"Well, I don't normally pull myself through a bathroom window. HEY!"

Arthur's belt was starting to slide loose.

"Watch out!" cried Buster.

"Don't let gooooooo!" wailed Francine.

Buster fell back with Arthur's belt as

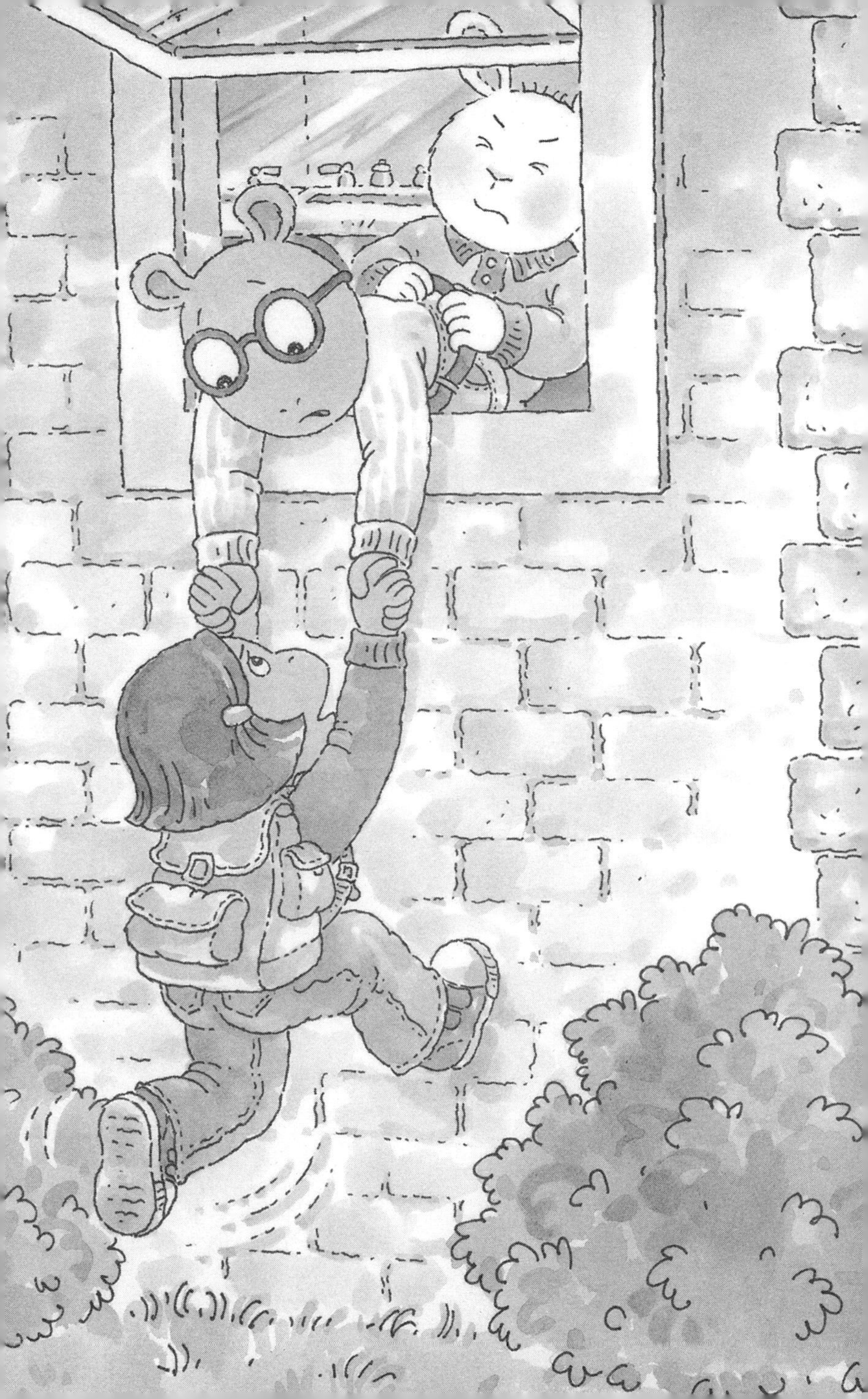

Arthur started to slide out the window. He grabbed the windowsill in time, but had to let go of Francine. She dropped down to the ground, back where she had started.

"Sorry," said Arthur.

Francine looked up angrily. "Now what?" she said.

"Need some help?"

Arthur and Buster whirled around to find Binky standing behind them. They explained what was happening.

Binky seemed very calm. "I know what to do," he said. "I saw it in a movie once." He leaned out the window.

"Leave it to me, Francine," he said. "I have a plan."

Chapter 7

· · · · · · · · · · ·

A short time later, Arthur and Buster were back in the classroom. Binky had described his plan to them, and while they had no reason to think it would work, neither of them had any better plan to put in its place.

"Whatever we do," said Arthur, rubbing his arms, "I'm not pulling Francine through any more windows."

Binky walked by them and tugged on his ear.

"Why did he do that?" asked Buster.

"Don't you remember?" said Arthur. "That's the signal."

"Why do we need a signal?" said Buster.

"That was in the movie, too."

"So what do we do after he makes the signal?" asked Buster.

"We wait," said Arthur.

Buster frowned. "For what?"

Suddenly Binky started screaming and hopping around on one foot.

"Ow! Ooooch! Hey! OWWW!"

While Mr. Ratburn hurried over to see what was the matter, Arthur and Buster tiptoed out of the room, past the principal's office, and toward the front door.

But Francine wasn't there.

"Where is she?" said Buster. "She's supposed to be here."

Arthur frowned. "I guess she didn't see the same movie Binky saw." He poked his head out the door and saw Francine standing way down the driveway, at a different door.

"Francine!" Arthur hissed. "Over here!"

She shook her head. "You're supposed to be over here!" she hissed back.

"No, no," Buster put in. "You're supposed to be —"

"I am not! You're supposed —"

The bell rang.

"Hurry up!" said Arthur. "Do you want to get inside the school or not? We don't have much time."

Meanwhile, Binky had moved out into the hall. He was still hopping but quickly getting tired.

Mr. Ratburn was watching him closely. "Do you require medical attention, Mr. Barnes?" he asked.

"Heh, heh," said Binky. "It's my shoe, Mr. Ratburn. Too tight, I guess."

"Then I suggest you get a new pair," said Mr. Ratburn.

Mr. Ratburn turned to go back in the classroom and noticed Arthur and Buster standing at the front door. They appeared to be yelling at someone outside.

"It must be the full moon," he muttered to himself, and headed toward them.

"No, wait!" cried Binky. "I think it's my socks. They're elastic! They hurt! You need to look at them."

But Mr. Ratburn was no longer listening. He was striding down the hall with Arthur and Buster, clearly in his sights.

"What's going on?" he asked, just as Francine slid inside the open door.

Arthur, Buster, and Francine turned to face him — and all started talking at once.

"It's not what you think."

"Well, it is, but not really."

"Actually, we can explain — I hope."

The commotion even brought Principal Haney out of his office.

"What's going on?" he asked.

"Francine, are you just getting to school?" Mr. Ratburn asked.

"I . . . uh . . . I . . . uh . . ."

Mr. Haney eyed the kids sternly. "I think you'd better all come to my office," he said. "That way we can get everything straightened out."

Chapter 8

• • • • • • • • • • •

Buster, Arthur, Binky, and Francine all sat outside Mr. Haney's office. None of them was sitting up very straight. Through the window, they could see Mr. Haney, Mr. Ratburn, and Francine's dad, Mr. Frensky, talking together. They didn't seem to be yelling or arguing, but then they didn't seem to be trading jokes, either.

Francine put her head in her hands. "I'm doomed. When I looked in Mr. Ratburn's eyes, my whole life passed before me."

"Did you see all the good parts?" asked Buster.

Francine sighed. "Puh-leeze. No more questions. The condemned prisoner usually gets a last meal. I bet I won't even get that."

"Not necessarily," said Buster. "I heard about this one girl who got expelled. But then she got a job selling doughnuts, and now she can eat as many as she wants without paying. That's even better than a last meal."

"I don't want to get a job," said Francine. "I'd rather go to school."

"Maybe they'll only expel you for a year," said Buster.

Arthur made a face at Buster and patted Francine on the shoulder. "Don't pay any attention to Buster," he said. "He's just exaggerating."

"He is?" asked Francine.

"Absolutely," said Arthur. "They would never expel you for being late."

Francine brightened a little. "That's a relief."

"They might make you come in early every day for a month to wash the lunchroom floor, but that —"

"Wash the floor? I don't want to wash floors."

"I don't blame you," said Binky. "They get pretty sticky."

"And the whole thing's really not your fault," said Arthur.

"You can say that again," said Francine. "It's your fault, Arthur. If you hadn't made me dare you, none of this would have happened!"

"Me? I didn't make anyone do anything. You're the one who —"

Before Arthur could protest further, Mr. Haney's door opened and everyone came out. Arthur was hoping that one of them might crack a little smile, but he had no such luck. Their stern faces might as well have been carved in stone.

Mr. Frensky spoke first. "I'm very disappointed in you, Francine," he said. "Where on earth did you get the idea to skip school?"

Francine glared at Arthur. "I . . . um . . . it just came to me, I guess." She slumped down on the bench. "My own stupid idea."

Mr. Haney cleared his throat. "Then I'm afraid you'll have to spend all of next week after school. I'm treating this as a warning, Francine, because you've never done anything like this before. However, I will not be so forgiving should this ever happen again."

"It won't," Francine said in a small voice.

"I'm also quite disappointed in you, Francine," said Mr. Ratburn.

"Which, I'm afraid, makes the disappointment unanimous," said her father.

"I'm sorry," said Francine, in a voice so small it could only have been heard by a mouse.

Chapter 9

· · · · · · · · · · ·

The matter had been settled. The judge had spoken and the prisoner had received her punishment. The whole thing was finished. Over.

At least most people would have looked at it that way. But not Arthur. "Wait!" he said. "This isn't fair. Francine wasn't the only one involved. It wasn't her idea to begin with. It was my idea."

"Oh?" said Mr. Haney.

"Oh?" said Mr. Ratburn and Mr. Frensky together.

"Uh-oh," said Buster, all by himself.

Francine said nothing, but she gave Arthur a grateful look.

"Only not exactly," Arthur went on. "I mean, I never meant it for real, and I don't think Francine did, either. The thing just took on a life of its own, like one of those monsters in those old sci-fi movies. You see, once the dare started, Brain said we had to do it, and there was no way to watch Dark Bunny and do our homework, because Mr. Ratburn had given us so much of it." He took a deep breath.

"So, Arthur, what are you trying to say exactly?" asked Mr. Haney. "And keep it brief."

Arthur stopped to think. "Just that, well, if Francine has to be punished, then I should be punished with her."

Buster stood up. "Arthur's right. Francine wasn't alone. I was there. The double dares sucked me in like a giant vacuum cleaner. Punish me, too."

"And me," said Binky, who was beginning to feel a little left out. "Don't forget me."

"But Binky," said Francine, "you weren't there yesterday when we dared each other. You didn't have anything to do with it."

"Oh, right." Binky waved his arms like an umpire calling the runner safe at second. "Forget me, then. Just forget me. Pretend I'm not here."

"Oh, I don't think we should do that entirely," Mr. Ratburn pointed out. "After all, Mr. Barnes, you did put on quite a display of fancy footwork. It wasted some valuable class time."

Binky's face reddened as he looked down at his shoes.

"But we were all involved," said Arthur. "That should count for something."

Mr. Ratburn exchanged a look with Mr. Haney. "I suppose it does," he said. "And

51

I applaud your spirit. But since you changed your mind and made it to school, you weren't late. So it makes no sense to punish you for that."

"But . . . but . . . ," Arthur began.

"However," Mr. Ratburn continued, "you did leave the classroom without permission. I also suspect that you failed to do your homework for today. Is that so?" Arthur and Buster nodded. In all the commotion, they had forgotten about that little detail.

"So," Mr. Ratburn continued, "for that infraction, I will give you each an extra assignment."

"Which is kind of like being punished," Buster whispered to Arthur.

Arthur nodded. And in this case, somehow, being punished made him feel much better. And he could tell from the look on Francine's face that it made her feel better, too.

Chapter 10

· · · · · · · · · · · · ·

Later that day, Mr. Ratburn entered the teacher's room and carefully closed the door. Once he was out of sight of any students, he permitted himself a small smile. One thing about third graders — they were never dull.

"Busy day, Rat?" asked Mr. Marco, who was grading some tests.

Mr. Ratburn nodded. "It had its moments. Did you bring the tape?"

Mr. Marco handed him a videotape, which Mr. Ratburn slid into the VCR in the corner. Then he sat down in a chair and pressed the remote control.

"I just don't understand," he said, "why good students would choose to skip school or fall behind on their homework." He shook his head. "They need to learn to plan ahead. Maybe I'll design a new unit for next quarter. . . ."

The tape came on.

"And now," said the TV announcer, "it's time to watch your favorite hare-y hero as he battles the Sixty-Foot Squid. I hope you're in your bathing suits, because that's the best way to enjoy the next ninety minutes of oceanic action!"

"All right!" said Mr. Ratburn. "This should be good."

"It's a great one," said Mr. Marco. "Wait till you see the giant clam. For something that lives in the water, it looks like it could use an industrial-strength bath. It's just absolutely disgusting, the way it sucks up Bunny and —"

"Sssssh!" said Mr. Ratburn, holding a finger to his lips. "Don't spoil the ending."